THE SWEETEST CHRISTMAS

Written by Ann Braybrooks
Cover by Don Williams
Interior Illustrations by Josie Yee

🐛 **A GOLDEN BOOK • NEW YORK**

Golden Books Publishing Company, Inc., New York, New York 10106

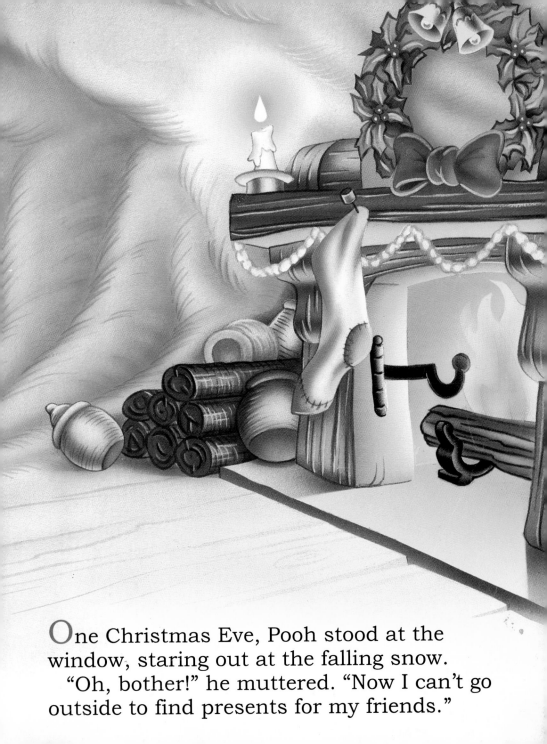

One Christmas Eve, Pooh stood at the
window, staring out at the falling snow.

"Oh, bother!" he muttered. "Now I can't go
outside to find presents for my friends."

"Think, think, think," thought Pooh. Then he brightened. "I know," he said. "I shall look *inside*."

Under his bed Pooh found a box. "Yo-yos would make nice Christmas presents," he said to himself. "But I suppose they would be more useful if they had strings."

Next, Pooh found some pinwheels in a drawer.
He blew on one pinwheel after another, but for
some reason none of them would spin.

"The wind must have worn these pinwheels out," he said.

Then Pooh noticed some marbles in a jar.

"I have eight friends," Pooh said happily to himself, "so I shall need eight marbles. One, two, three . . . four, five, six. Six? Oh, stuff and fluff. I don't have enough."

Pooh slumped in a chair. "Think, think, think," he said. "What would *I* want for Christmas?"

Just then Pooh's tummy rumbled. "I know!" he cried. "HONEY!"

Pooh hurried to his cupboard and counted his honey pots. "Eight," he said, frowning, "which means there wouldn't be any left for me."

Pooh thought and thought. Finally he declared, "I *do* want to give my friends something wonderful. So honey it must be."

Pooh waited for the snow to stop falling.
Then he loaded all eight honey pots onto his
sled and headed for Piglet's house.

When Piglet opened the door, Pooh handed him a pot of honey. "Merry Christmas, Piglet!" cried Pooh.

"Merry Christmas, Pooh!" replied Piglet. And he handed Pooh a gift, too.

At Owl's, Pooh delivered another pot of honey. "Merry Christmas, Owl!" said Pooh.

"Merry Christmas, Pooh!" said Owl. "I have a present for you, too. My Aunt Beazy—Beatrice, that is—collected it last spring."

"Why, thank you, Owl!" Pooh said politely.
Then he hurried on to see Rabbit.

Next, Pooh gave Rabbit a pot of honey, and Rabbit gave Pooh a gift in return.

"Oh, Rabbit," cried Pooh. "You shouldn't have!"

"Oh, yes, I should," grumbled Rabbit. "Now maybe you won't eat mine!"

Then Eeyore and Pooh exchanged presents. "Fancy that," said Eeyore. "One for me, and one for you. I'm going to have this honey with thistles. Thank you, Pooh."

Pooh headed for Kanga's house.

On the way he ran into Christopher Robin. "I'm delivering Christmas presents to my friends," Pooh told him, "but I had to use up all my honey."

"Oh, Pooh!" said Christopher Robin. "I have a wonderful idea. You go on to Kanga's, and I'll see you soon."

When Pooh arrived at Kanga's house, he
found Tigger with Kanga and Roo.
"Merry Christmas, everyone!" said Pooh.

While Pooh was giving his friends their pots of honey, Christopher Robin hurried in with a large box.

"Tigger, Kanga, and Roo have something for you, Pooh," said the boy. "Why don't you open all your presents now?"

Pooh's surprise grew as he unwrapped one
pot of honey after another. Finally he opened
the large box from Christopher Robin. Inside
were five *more* honey pots!

"Merry Christmas, Pooh!" said
Christopher Robin. "You've been such a
generous bear, such a kind bear, that you
deserve pots and pots of honey!"

"Oh, thank you!" exclaimed Pooh as he helped himself to a smackerel. "Mmm," he said, licking his lips. "What a very sweet Christmas this is!"